Mucky Pup's Christmas

For Janice

First published in Great Britain by Andersen Press Ltd in 1998
First published in Picture Lions in 1999
1 3 5 7 9 10 8 6 4 2
ISBN: 0 00 6646867
Text and illustrations © copyright Ken Brown 1998
The author/illustrator asserts the moral right to be
identified as the author/illustrator of the work.
Picture Lions is an imprint of the Children's Division,
part of HarperCollins Publishers Ltd,
77-85 Fulham Palace Road, Hammersmith, London, W6 8JB.
The HarperCollins website address is:
www.fireandwater.com
Printed in Hong Kong.

Mucky Pup's Christmas

KEN BROWN

PictureLions

An Imprint of HarperCollinsPublishers

Mucky Pup was busy being helpful.
He collected the post, sampled the cake,

and rearranged the tree.

Clever Mucky Pup!

No-one else thought he was clever.
　"Bad, *bad* Mucky Pup! You've spoilt
the Christmas cards."
　"You've spoilt the Christmas cake."
　"You've spoilt the Christmas tree."
　"And it's Christmas tomorrow! Out! Out of the house!"

Mucky Pup went to find Pig.

"What's up?" said Pig.
"They don't want me," said Mucky Pup miserably.
"They say I've spoilt this Christmas thing.
Do you know what it is, Pig?"

Pig didn't know.
Nor did Horse or Hen or Duck.
Cat *said* she knew but wasn't telling.
     "It doesn't sound much fun whatever it is,"
          said Pig. "Cheer up, Mucky Pup.
          Stay here with us tonight."

So Mucky Pup snuggled down in the soft, warm straw with Pig. He thought he could hear someone calling his name, but perhaps it was just a dream.

The next morning, everything
was clean and white and new.

"Do you think it's the Christmas thing,
Pig?" asked Mucky Pup.

"Can't be," said Pig. "It looks too much fun.
Come on, Mucky Pup. Let's play!"

And that's what they did...

They skated,

they snowballed,

they sledged and...

Wheeeeeeee...

"Mucky Pup! *Clever* Mucky Pup, you found us!

We've called and called. Don't you know?
It's Christmas Day!"

And they put him on the sled and went back
to the warm, bright house, where Mucky Pup
at last found out what Christmas was.
There were parcels, and paper,
and his very own present...

... and it was *lots* of fun.

"I didn't spoil Christmas after all,"
thought Mucky Pup happily.
"I shall tell Pig tomorrow!"

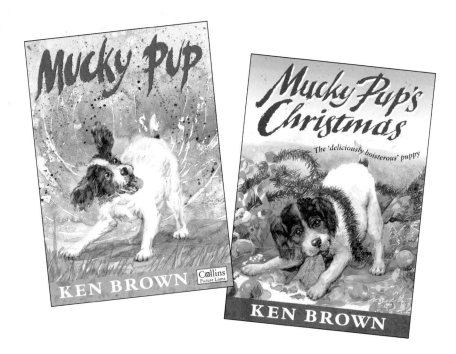

Mucky Pup's Christmas is the second book about this adorable puppy. In the first title, *Mucky Pup*, he is looking for someone to play with but everyone thinks he is just too mucky. Everyone, that is, until he meets Pig who loves to get mucky just as much as Pup does!

Mucky Pup was shortlisted for the Kate Greenaway Medal and the character was described in *Junior Education* as 'deliciously boisterous'.